I0649688

The Beast
Of
Archer Hall

Introduction

"I chased the devil,
I stared into the

darkness at the heart of this city. When others would have chose to turn and run from what lives in the shadows I instead pushed forward. Almost, instinctively I ran head first into flames not once considering the possibility that I might get burned. Maybe I was naive to think a badge was some form of shield, that somehow protected me or the people I loved from the devils touch. Like a fool I chased after the devil, and now he has found me"

Those were the last words of my father, but will they be mine?

Episode 1

Tonight I can almost smell the rust on this old, run down fire escape. What's it been, ten, eleven years now? I remember the day my dad first bought this dump of an apartment. He had just made detective which came with a pay increase, although you couldn't tell by how shabby this place was when we first moved in. Gosh, I had just turned six years old back then. My mom was a wreck, dealing with my younger sister who was four at the time, while pregnant with my little brother, luckily I was able to take care of myself. As far back as I can remember I have always been taking care of myself, the life of a cops daughter is an independent one, besides my mom had enough on her plate, and since my father was always on the job, it was just better for everyone that I just stayed to myself. I hate this fire escape, I hate this apartment, and most of all I hate this city, this city that stole my father from me, its like it was just yesterday that he was here telling me stories about the different cases he would be working on, although extremely watered down versions excluding any r-rated details. Still, it was engaged in those conversations and listening to his stories I realized how much I wanted to be just like him. My father lived as a hero, but thanks to this city he died a broken man, so why do I want to stay here? It can't be for my friends whom I haven't spoken to since my father died, maybe, maybe its because I want to be reminded day in and day out of who my father was, and how much he meant to me since this hurt, this pain, is all I have left of him now. It has only been a year now since his death, everyday I watch as my sister and brother go about their lives as if they have already forgotten him, but worse then them is my mother, how could she move on so fast? Without missing a beat she sold most of his stuff, and what little she kept was only cause I begged her to, now she wants us to move? One random phone call, from some estate lawyer telling her a great uncle she never met has died, and where moving clear across the state to a town I never even heard of, Maybe its karma? A few weeks before she received that random phone call I was telling her how I wished she had died instead of my dad during and argument, I didn't mean it, but, I just can't act like them, I can't put on a fake smile and go about my life as if nothing happened, I loved my dad, our family, and this dump of an apartment in this filthy crime ridden city, I just don't know how to express that to my mom, every time she speaks to me I get so upset, and I end up blowing up at her. Vigil City, is this it? Are we finally through? Will you remember me? Alyssa Glass, daughter of

Detective Martin Glass, the man you destroyed, or was my family just some insignificant spec of dust in this dead soulless city? I guess, I'm moving to Archer Hall.

There's a chill in the air tonight, has it really been a year since my parents died? My father whom I thought was invincible. Who's shadow seemed to immense to ever escape, he was a stern man, at times very hard to live with, he had a way of making any and all joy completely evaporate from a room as soon as he entered it. I feared my father, and that fear made me respect him. My whole life has been a failed attempt at earning his approval, trying to somehow prove I'm deserving of the Blackwell name. Even in death it seems I'm trying to honor my duty as his progeny, or else I would have left this cursed town, since I could talk I have asked myself what am I doing here, Why would anyone choose to live in Archer Hall? This town and everyone in it, are rotten, my mother was the only good thing this town had to offer, she was beautiful, with hair as gold as the sun, and as long as time, her eyes were like blue diamonds, and her smile was as warm as a summer day, I remember her holding me as a kid, I felt so safe and happy in her arms, she made being my fathers son almost bearable, so why couldn't i just be content? Why did I have to tell her I was leaving her and Archer Hall? I remember that day like it was yesterday, the day before my parents died, the fight we had, and the last thing I ever got to say to them. I told them I was leaving Archer Hall, of course this infuriated my father, he had big plans for me after all, my life was mapped out at birth, no, during the conception of the idea of a Blackwell heir, he had planned out my entire existence. My mother argued that the world outside of this town was dangerous, but now I know the truth, I have seen the face of the true evil of this town and I'm trapped in its web, I don't regret wanting to leave this place, even if it would mean leaving my mother, the only person I have ever loved or cared about behind, I only regret telling my parents that I would rather die then stay in Archer Hall, those were my last words to them, I stormed off on my motorcycle, feeling so full of myself, here I was telling them I could make it on my own, then riding off on the motorcycle my father bought me, looking back I acted like nothing more then a spoiled child, they chased after me and died in a car crash, or so I was told, I don't actually remember all that much about how that day ended, the last thing I remember, I was racing out of Archer Hall, into the neighboring town of Gravesdale next thing I knew, I was waking up in my family estate to my families personal physician telling me my parents died in a car accident and I crashed my motorcycle, in that moment I was to out of it to think straight, let alone feel anything for what my physician had just told me. Since then however, I can't stop thinking about it. What really happened? How could me and my parents both end up in accidents? One thing was clear though, my parents were dead because of me, now I'm alone in this Nag forsaken town, the last of the cursed Blackwell bloodline, Ethan Blackwell, heir to a dynasty I never wanted, I guess I'm stuck in Archer Hall.

Holy crap tonight is dead, there isn't a thing interesting coming through this police scanner, how is a girl supposed to write a good story with nothing exciting to report on? I can't keep writing these puff pieces, and this gossip trash on my blog, true Greenworks fans want hard hitting journalism, man I miss the city, back when me and my dad lived in Gridlock there was always something going on, some angle to investigate for a story,

those were the days,
back when my father
was a journalist, a
true journalist, who
lived for a good story,
corrupt politicians,
gangsters and dirty
cops alike, feared the
name Walter Green,
because they knew if
my dad was onto you,
that meant anything
you did in the dark
was about to come to
light, It's been five

years since we moved to this boring little town, after my father decided to pursue a career as a crime novelist, this career change came after he and my step mom got married, it isn't like I hate her, I don't even dislike her, She is pretty great all things considered, and she makes him happy, I just miss back when it was just me and him, My mom died in labor with me, so all I ever knew was a life with just the two of us, I remember the all nighters, Where he would stay up for hours writing, listening to police scanners, and rushing out to crime scenes, since he didn't trust the public school system I was home schooled, and spent everyday with him working his cases, guess what else changed when he got married and we moved to Archer Hall? Its official, my dad is domesticated, that hard edge, that grit he used to have, that made him a great journalist, its gone, Walter Green is just a husband and father with a daughter obsessed with investigative journalism. I miss Gridlock, I can remember it like it was yesterday, the city was alive, it had its own personality, It wasn't the prettiest city, it was tough, most importantly it was my city, it was in that city, by my fathers side, I realized how much I loved journalism, I inherited his hunger for the truth, and his passion for writing, sadly, all I can write about here is the daily drama at Archer Hall Academy, there is this one story I'm working on, Although, its more conspiracy theories then a fleshed out story at this point, gosh I wish we never

moved to Archer Hall
but here I am,
Elizabeth Green,
unknown high school
journalist.

Can't sleep again
tonight, working out
doesn't seem to help
either, no matter how
much I punch this
heavy bag, or how

many weights I lift, I can't burn off this energy, or shake this uneasy feeling I have, there's something in the air tonight, change is coming to Archer Hall, I can sense it, or better yet smell it, the scent of blood is in the air, as far back as I can remember I have had a nose for these kinds of things, my father called it chiming, he had it, and his father before him, the story goes, sons of the Knight bloodline were born to be protectors of the innocent, chiming came in handy for that purpose, it allowed men of Knight lineage to vibrate on a different frequency then other people, this sixth sense was said to be triggered by the winds, different winds for different circumstances, but only three in total, the wind of the past allowed us to see into the history of any person place or thing, the wind of the present allowed us to see beyond the veil most others don't even know exist, lastly the wind of the future allowed us to glimpse into whats to come, of these so called winds, I have experienced none, just a great bedtime story I guess. I can remember my father telling me that story when I was a kid like it was yesterday, those stories were the only times my father ever really spoke to me, other than to

scold me, I was never
good enough, and
nothing I did could
change that, he
pushed me into
sports, but not once
attended a single
event, I have been
winning trophies since
I could walk, and still
finding time to make
sure to be top of my
class academically,
my mother would tell
me he just doesn't

know how to show
how much he truly
loves me, however, I
have always known
the truth, he has
always hated me, two
years left of high
school and I will be
out of his hair, I will
put Archer Hall in my
rearview and never
look back, theres
nothing here for me
in this town, and I
refuse to end up like

my father, oddly
enough most kids
assume being the son
of the town sheriff
means they would be
able to do whatever
they wanted with no
consequences, in
reality its hell,
everyone has and
opinion of how you
should behave, every
aspect of your life is
scrutinized, worst of
all are the people in

this town, to be judged and looked down upon, by these people. My name is James Knight, and I truly despise Archer Hall

Today is the day, the last day I would see my south Vigil apartment, or Vigil city period for that matter, the movers left with the last of the stuff we had here, so it wouldn't be long before my mom came into my room calling me in off my fire escape, to set out on a three hour trip to the town of Archer Hall, what should I do? Its not like I haven't thought of running away, but thats just anger talking, I love my family, I just don't know how to be

around them now,
I'm always angry, I
want to be normal
again, I want to smile
and mean it, but until
then I guess I have to
put on a fake smile, I
refuse to look weak,
or allow anyone to
think I'm not in
control, like I'm losing
my mind, or going
crazy like they say my
father did.

Samantha Glass;
"hey, Lyssa, its time
to head out"

I didn't even hear her
come in my room, or
should I say this
room, guess its
goodbye fire escape,
chin up, smile,

because everyone is watching.

Alyssa Glass; "okay mom, I'll be right out"

As I wiped my eyes and climbed into my room from the fire escape for the last time, I knew the girl I was could never come back, I had to move forward and find out who I was now, or who I would become. I made my way downstairs to the car, everyone looking so eager to hit the road, it was sickening, but new day new me right? From here on out Alyssa was gonna be all smiles.

This house is so cold, if it weren't for my servants I would truly be alone here, I guess I should get ready for the day, so often now I find myself unwilling to get out of bed, but someone has to uphold the Blackwell name, so a fake smile acts as my shield blocking anyone from seeing how I'm truly feeling. Tomorrow will be my first day back at school since my parents died, I can't appear weak, those who hate me and my lineage will never find joy in my pain.

Butler; "young master you have a guest downstairs"

Ethan Blackwell;
"huh, oh, its you, I
didn't hear you come
in, I will be down in a
moment"

Butler; "alright sir,
and I'm sorry if I
startled you"

Ethan Blackwell; "its
fine, I wasn't startled
just caught off guard"

I wonder who could be here to see me, and why? Death has a way of bringing out the worst people you forgot you knew, and seeing as my parents left me a billion dollar fortune, everyone I forgot I knew seem to keep popping up. As I started heading downstairs I realized this person I forgot I knew was the worst of them all, Gisselle Blackwell, my cousin and tormentor for most of my early childhood, she is a sadistic sociopath and she's only in middle school.

Ethan Blackwell; "Gisselle, what brings you here?"

Gisselle Blackwell; "I start high school tomorrow, so I wanted to give you a heads up that I'm enrolled in Archer Hall Academy"

Ethan Blackwell; "is that all?"

Gisselle Blackwell;
"nice poker face,
you're definitely
gonna need it"

This girl is psychotic,
I can't show any
emotion around her,
and yet I feel anger
burning inside me, I
have to end this
conversation now.

Ethan Blackwell;
"well if thats all, see
you around"

Gisselle Blackwell; "so
your parents are
really dead huh?"

There she is, her
fangs on full display,
but I expected this, in
fact this is kinda a
poor attempt at
eliciting a response.

Ethan Blackwell;
"Brewl teaches us, no
one ever really dies,
we only return to the
infinite black"

Gisselle Blackwell;
"yeah, you really do
have a great poker
face"

This girl is going to be
a problem…

Gosh, James is late again, how the hell are we supposed to break any story when we are always late to the scene? I have a good feeling about this one, reports coming through my scanner are saying there was an animal attack in the middle of a parking lot outside a bar resulting in a fatality, sounds way more than just a little fishy, a random animal prowling bar parking lots to attack and kill people? I can't believe people are so blind.

Dam, I'm late, Elle's gonna kill me, why the hell did I even agree to help her with this nonsense, well, maybe its cause she's so freaking cute but

still, chasing behind
my father at different
crime scenes isn't how
I envisioned spending
my Sunday night.

Finally, he's here…

Well, I'm here…

Elizabeth Green; "bro
what took you so
long? There isn't

gonna be anything left at the crime scene"

James Knight; "crime scene? Look its just an animal attack"

Elizabeth Green; "please don't pretend to be a sheep, I know you've been noticing the strange shit that happens in this town"

James Knight; "look I admit this town is strange, unlike you I actually lived here my whole life, so I can't deny its weird, but you're imagination.." Elizabeth Green; "my imagination is exactly what this small town needs"

Dam she's so fucking cute…

Elizabeth Green; "why are you looking at me like that? You should watch the road"

She's right I should watch the road, its just ever since she came to this town I've been drawn to her, hell she might even be right about this town needing her imagination, because I know I sure do, she makes everyday bearable.

Seems like we are almost to the bar, hmm, why does James stare at me all the time? Note to self, must investigate further.

James Knight; "look Elle, there could be officers still around so lets keep our heads down"

Elizabeth Green; "we aren't gonna break any news from the sidelines, get in the game James, hey that rhymed"

James Knight;
"Adorable"

Elizabeth Green;
"what?"

James Knight; "I
meant affordable, like,
we can't afford to get
in any trouble, matter
fact, lets just go
already"

That was close, I hope I played that off…

Did he just call me adorable? Note to self, investigate further…

What happened next was unexpected, Elle rushed over to the crime scene, luckily the body had been removed from the scene and all evidence was collected, however there was still enough to see to spark Elle's imagination. Scratches in the concrete like something out of a horror movie, too large to be a normal animal, and a pool of blood with a trail of large prints that almost resemble a sloths paw prints, three large nails on each paw, but the craziest part is right before the prints reach the street they stop, followed by human foots prints continuing to the street. She was ecstatic, she had found proof that something unexplainable was definitely going on, but I felt something lot different from ecstasy, there was a chill in the air, I could feel whatever kill this person was watching us.

James Knight; "Elle its time to go"

Elizabeth Green; "go? Do you know what we found we have to take pics and post…"

James Knight; "fine, take your pics then we are leaving"

Elizabeth Green; "are you ok? Is it the blood? I mean yeah I know it might be hard being around somewhere where someone.."

James Knight; "its not the blood, or death, or anything like that, I just need to get you out of here"

Elizabeth Green; "ok, just a few pics"

She truly is adorable watching her rush to get the perfect shots before we had to leave almost took away from the feeling that death was watching us.

Elizabeth Green;
"there, all done, we can official head back to my place and start blogging"

James Knight;
"Perfect, lets go"

I won't lie, I was scared, which made the speed limit irrelevant, I had to protect her at all cost. Elizabeth Green; "um, you're going a little fast don't you think?"

James Knight; "...."

Elizabeth Green;
"um, okay"

The further we got
from that place the
slower I began to
drive, yet I still
couldn't shake the
uneasy feeling I had.
Right when I thought
I could relax
something slammed
into the side of the car

causing me to spin out, when the car finally came to a stop we were in the middle of a backroad surrounded by woods, everything was pitch black except what could be seen by the head lights.

Elizabeth Green;
"what the fuck, what
was that?"

James Knight; "I
don't know, stay put,
I'm gonna check it
out"

Elizabeth Green;
"stay put? I'm gonna
check it out? Are you

crazy? This isn't some dumb ass generic horror movie where we make cliche movie mistakes, put this fucking car in drive and lets get out of here"

So yeah, I tried that, and like a cliche horror movie we had a blown tire...

James Knight; "the tires blown, I gotta change it or we aren't going anywhere"

Elizabeth Green; "why the fuck not? To hell with a blown tire, drive on that shit till the rim gone"

This girl, I couldn't stop laughing, here I was in a kinda terrifying situation, and yet she helped me relax.

James Knight; "don't worry Elle, I would never let anything happen to you"

Why does he always look at me like that, and why do I always feel so, I don't know, when he does, note to self, investigate further…

Elizabeth Green; "just be careful"

James Knight; "always"

Always? When did he get so, I don't know…

As soon as I got out the car I knew something was off, there was no sign of what hit us, and Elle's door was completely dented in from where whatever rammed us, but the scary part was the tire was shredded, and deep claw marks were carved into the rim, something purposely stranded us here. I didn't know what to do or say, I couldn't let Elle see me panic because that would cause her to panic, so I found myself replaying in my head shit my father taught me as a kid, its funny where your mind wonders in tense situations, I took a deep breath, like he taught me, and closed my eyes to see with my minds eye, I listened to the wind like so many times before, so many times where I ended up seeing nothing at all, but this time, I saw something horrifying, a woman covered in matted grey fur, with long sloth like arms and claws the size of butcher knives, her face was both animalistic and humanoid, she was covered in blood and crouched down in the tree right in front of me.

To be continued…

www.ingramcontent.com/pod-product-compliance
Lightning Source LLC
Chambersburg PA
CBHW051527050726
47503CB00014B/2179

9781737186588